For Paula and David
without whom....
you're a gorgeous couple
and it's ~~been~~ a delight
getting to know you
———— all ~~through~~ a dragon
and a Scouse mouse

love

ARBello
x

22 Oct 2003

The Dragon That Squeaked

Adventures of the dragon who *lives* in St George's Hall

by

Arabella McIntyre-Brown

illustrated by Liverpool children:

Amanda Childs, Guy Cohen, Alex Cook, Tom Currie,
Steve Daly, Ashleigh Despoti, Lauren Duckworth,
Mary Edgar, Gemma Fearon, Leigh Fitzpatrick,
Natalie Fowler, Paul Gibson, Olivia Hansen-Bruder,
Kaine Jones, James Killick, Peter King, Paul Lee,
Lacey Littlemore, Thomas McDonough, Suzanne Morris,
Caitlin Murney, Tommy Newman, Oliver Padget,
Vlad Paraoan, Andrew Price, Helen Robertshaw,
Callum Strode, Danielle Ward, Sophie Wilson

garlic
PRESS

The Dragon That Squeaked

Adventures of the dragon who lives in St George's Hall

Written by Arabella McIntyre-Brown

Illustrated by Liverpool children:

Amanda Childs, Guy Cohen, Alex Cook, Tom Currie, Steve Daly, Ashleigh Despoti, Lauren Duckworth, Mary Edgar, Gemma Fearon, Leigh Fitzpatrick, Natalie Fowler, Paul Gibson, Olivia Hansen-Bruder, Kaine Jones, James Killick, Peter King, Paul Lee, Lacey Littlemore, Thomas McDonough, Suzanne Morris, Caitlin Murney, Tommy Newman, Oliver Padgett, Vlad Paraoan, Andrew Price, Helen Robertshaw, Callum Strode, Danielle Ward, Sophie Wilson

Cover design by Ken Ashcroft; illustration workshops by Marie Mairs; photography by Guy Woodland; proofreading by Judy Tasker; printed and bound in Spain by Bookprint SL

ISBN 1-904099-04-1

First published in 2003 by Garlic Press Publishing Ltd

71 Prenton Road West, Birkenhead, CH42 9PZ
Tel +44 (0)151 608 7006
email: dragons@garlicpress.co.uk
www.garlicpress.co.uk

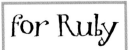

for Ruby

foreword
by David Swift

A Liverpool childhood is an incomparable privilege which both my wife Paula and I were lucky enough to enjoy. The city's buccaneering, entrepreneurial, artistic, seafaring, picaresque, cosmopolitan, deprived-but-dignified past has produced generations of vital, entertaining, go-getting visionaries and pioneers in all fields: business, art, entertainment, the law, politics, medicine, academe, sport, the services and more.

And now from the animal kingdom – breathing invigorating Mersey air and inhabiting the great St George's Hall (the finest neo-classical building in Europe and one of the most important buildings in the world), we have two new Liverpudlian heroes – Gezza the mouse and Xiaolong the squeaking dragon, created by Arabella McIntyre-Brown in her captivating panoramic historic tale of the city.

The JP Jacobs Charitable Trust was established by my wife's late father Phill Jacobs (a passionate Scouser and a product of Liverpool Institute and Gwladys Road Stand, Goodison Park), with a continuing policy of funding Merseyside children's projects. The Trustees are absolutely delighted that the Trust's help has enabled this enchanting book, illustrated colourfully and imaginatively by 29 local schoolchildren, to be published.

The Trustees are thrilled that as well as selling the book to raise funds for the restoration campaign, St George's Hall can give a copy of *The Dragon That Squeaked* to every school student in Liverpool in Years Four, Five and Six as part of the Capital of Culture's Year of Learning.

Chapter 1

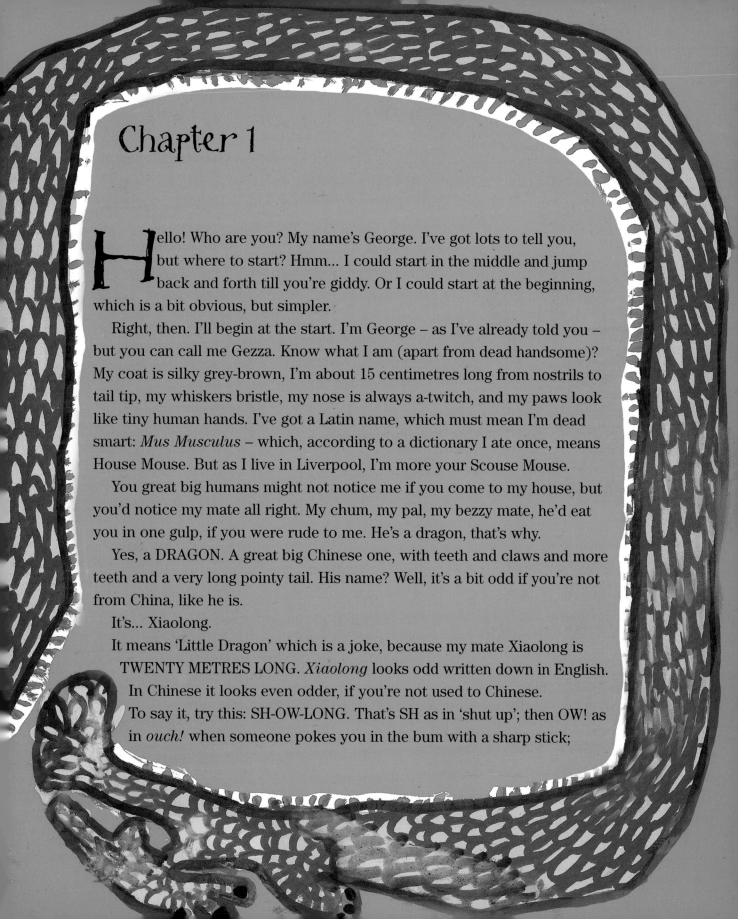

Hello! Who are you? My name's George. I've got lots to tell you, but where to start? Hmm... I could start in the middle and jump back and forth till you're giddy. Or I could start at the beginning, which is a bit obvious, but simpler.

Right, then. I'll begin at the start. I'm George – as I've already told you – but you can call me Gezza. Know what I am (apart from dead handsome)? My coat is silky grey-brown, I'm about 15 centimetres long from nostrils to tail tip, my whiskers bristle, my nose is always a-twitch, and my paws look like tiny human hands. I've got a Latin name, which must mean I'm dead smart: *Mus Musculus* – which, according to a dictionary I ate once, means House Mouse. But as I live in Liverpool, I'm more your Scouse Mouse.

You great big humans might not notice me if you come to my house, but you'd notice my mate all right. My chum, my pal, my bezzy mate, he'd eat you in one gulp, if you were rude to me. He's a dragon, that's why.

Yes, a DRAGON. A great big Chinese one, with teeth and claws and more teeth and a very long pointy tail. His name? Well, it's a bit odd if you're not from China, like he is.

It's... Xiaolong.

It means 'Little Dragon' which is a joke, because my mate Xiaolong is TWENTY METRES LONG. *Xiaolong* looks odd written down in English. In Chinese it looks even odder, if you're not used to Chinese. To say it, try this: SH-OW-LONG. That's SH as in 'shut up'; then OW! as in *ouch!* when someone pokes you in the bum with a sharp stick;

then LONG, which is easy. SH-OW-LONG.

But on paper, in an English book, it's spelt XIAOLONG.

And here's the funniest thing about Xiaolong, the huge big Chinese Dragon. What do you think a dragon's voice is like? Deep, fierce, loud, rumble, roar, yes? No. Not my dragon. My dragon has a different voice. He... er... squeaks. He can roar and rumble, but he usually squeaks, and in a Scouse accent, too. A bit like me. In fact, exactly like me. You see, Xiaolong learned how to speak my language from mice (from my ancestors, actually) so I suppose he thought that's how he had to do it. Squeakily. Scousily. It's weird, I can tell you, hearing a dragon squeak Scouse.

'Roar, Xiaolong. Rumble!' I tell him.

'Eeeeeey, Gezza, la,' he says in a squeak, 'it just doesn't sound right!'

What can you do with an enormous dragon that squeaks? I ask you...

* * *

Xiaolong and I live in a beautiful huge enormous vast great big gigantic large building in the middle of Liverpool, half way up Britain on the left (or on the North West coast of England, if you're any good at geography). The building is called St George's Hall, and it's famous.

Of course Xiaolong has lived here a bit longer than me, because he's a bit older. Well, in one way we're about the same age: he's 34 and I'm 32, but we count birthdays a bit differently, Xiaolong and me. So you understand, us mice live short lives compared to humans. We have about 15 birthdays in one human year, so in human time I'm only two. Confusing, isn't it?

But
dragons live a
long, long, long, long,
long, long, long, long, long, long, long, long,
long, long time. One single dragon year equals 60 human years, and 900 mouse years. So Xiaolong has lived 2,040 human years (that's almost two MILLION mouse years!!) already and he's not even fully-grown yet. Wow!

If you think THAT's impressive, wait till you see him. Do you know what a Chinese dragon looks like?

Most people in Europe think 'dragon' and get a picture in their mind of a horrible dirty big spiky thing with leathery wings, red eyes, rows of huge teeth and VERY bad breath. Dragons in Europe breathe fire, crunch up farms full of cows and sheep, kidnap truckloads of innocent maidens, trash whole villages, live in deep dark smelly caves, and are generally not very nice.

Chinese dragons, on the other hand, are altogether better neighbours. For starters, they don't breathe fire. They like water instead, and look after things rather than crunching them up. Chinese dragons are beautiful, their bodies are brilliant colours and their eyes shine like jewels, and they fly, twisting and tumbling in the clouds. They like to live by water, and some have gorgeous palaces at the bottom of lakes or rivers.

Xiaolong doesn't have a palace under water, but St George's Hall is like a palace, and we've got a whacking great river – the Mersey – just down the hill, and from the roof you can see the Irish Sea.

You're wondering how a Chinese dragon gets to live in Liverpool, aren't you? Well, I'll tell you.

Way back in the 1840s (when your great-great-great-great-great-great-grand-parents were alive), the wealthy music-lovers of Liverpool decided they needed a new concert hall, so they looked for an architect to design them something

smart. They chose a young man called Harvey (his full name was Harvey Lonsdale Elmes, so let's stick to Harvey), who came up with a gobsmacking great building overlooking the city centre and the river.

Then the legal big-wigs said they needed a new building for the law courts, and they asked Harvey to design them something too, right next door to the new concert hall. So he did. Then everyone realised they could save time and money if they built one huge great building with the law courts and the concert hall all under one roof. So they did.

Harvey got to work, and with the help of hundreds of stonemasons, bricklayers, engineers, errand boys, carpenters, plasterers, joiners, plumbers, labourers, glaziers, tea ladies, ironmasters, surveyors, painters, seamstresses, wheelbarrow-pushers, cart-drivers, ditch-diggers, foremen, gang leaders and accountants (there are always accountants), they built the hall. Even with everyone working their socks off, it still took 14 years to get everything done.

Now – this is where we come in – they needed silk to make some of the curtains and hangings, and the best silk in those days came by sea all the way from China.

Can you guess what happened? (One thing I should mention here is that Chinese dragons can change size: they can be big as the whole world or as small as a silkworm.)

I'll let Xiaolong tell you about the day in 1850 when he left China...

Chapter 2

'It was a Spring day and I had travelled from my home in the cool mountain lake, down through the racing waters of the Yangtze River to Shanghai, the city by the sea; I'd had a little nap over the winter months and was feeling peckish for seafood.

When the river reaches the city it is wide and deep, rich and cloudy with the salty tide; I waited till nightfall then came up to the surface in the harbour, among hundreds of boats as small as my foot, and dozens of ships twice as long as me. Even at night people were scurrying everywhere, shouting orders and chattering in groups. Cargoes waited on shore to be carried to every corner of the world: wooden crates and soft bundles that gave off scents of cedar and cinnamon, roses and ginger.

One ship lay quietly, a strange foreign ship with a man on the foredeck, standing guard in the light of a swaying lantern. The scents wafting from its portholes were irresistible, and I decided to climb aboard for a look around. Making myself small as a sea snake, I climbed the anchor chain, dropped to the deck and hurried across to an open hatch. I stuck my head into the opening and breathed in the perfumes and spices from the cargo.

Suddenly there were thuds and crashes as men leapt on to deck, shouting, laughing and cursing as they jumped about. Startled, I fell through the hatch on to something soft, and before I could change back to dragon size and give them all a fright, the hatch cover was banged shut and I was trapped in the pitch black hold. Trapped!

I felt the ship sway as the sails were hoisted and it got under way. All I could do was to listen to the creaking of ropes and shoosh of water, the crack of canvas and the hubbub of voices. I'd wait till we were out to sea,

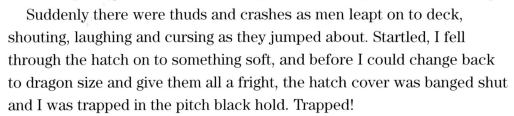

I thought, then make my escape. I curled up on a bale of silk and fell asleep.

I was woken by a clatter and a crash as the hatch cover was thrown open and two men climbed down into the hold. As they worked, I climbed out on deck to dive into the sea and swim away. The ship had docked in another harbour, but this was not China – the hot dry air burned my scales, the sea water smelled all wrong, and the sky was a different colour.

Deciding to wait till the ship returned to Chinese waters, I went back to my bale of silk, made myself the size of a silkworm, and burrowed right inside where I could sleep undisturbed till we got home.

The next thing I knew I was being shaken about and then there was a blinding light and a shriek. I was flung into the air and landed with a smash on a hard, cold floor. I lay stunned for a while before I realised what had happened. The bale of silk had been unrolled and a human woman, thinking I was some common worm, had thrown me off.

But where was this? It was damp and dusty; everything smelled foreign and I couldn't recognise anything. I was no longer at sea; this was not a ship but a building, strange, not like any place I'd seen before. The light was grey – where was the sun? I could smell salt but I could hear nothing of the ocean. I was lost, and every instinct told me that this was not a place for dragons.

Not wanting a fight, I stayed small and crept away to find a place I could hide and weep for my lost Chinese home. I followed the scent of water, down and down, through strange man-built caverns and tunnels, till I found a dark place where water trickled down the living rock into a small pool. I slid into the water and curled up at the bottom of the pool, weeping salty tears until I slept.'

Chapter 3

Hello, it's me again – Gezza. So, there he was, our dragon Xiaolong, stuck a million zillion miles from home without a friend in the world. Which is where we came in – us, the mice, my family. The very first creature to meet the visitor was my ancestor, George I. That's George the First – which is what he got called after he died because he was the very first Dragon Friend.

I'll explain more about that later. My official name is George LXIII, or George the 63rd if you don't know how to count in Roman numerals like I do. (I've explained them at the bottom of the page.)

Before I took over the job, there were 62 Georges before me, looking after Xiaolong. The thing is, you see, that he thinks there's only ever been one mouse. Can you believe it? But don't forget – a mouse lives about 900 years to every one dragon year, so we come and go too fast for him to keep up. We gave up trying to explain after several mouse generations, so we gave in and we all pretend we're still the original George. Well, it IS confusing, isn't it?

Let's go back to that day in 1850. What have we got: a Chinese dragon hiding at the bottom of a pool at the bottom of the basement of the biggest tallest newest building in the most important city in the whole world. OK, except maybe for London, but Liverpool was... what was that scrumptious word I chewed off page 387 of that dictionary?... pre-eminent, that's it. Liverpool was pre-eminent in world trade in those days, and everyone who was anyone came here: kings, queens, emperors, emirs, czars, sultans, rajas, pashas,

ROMAN NUMERALS			
I	1	X	10
II	2	XX	20
III	3	XL	40
IV	4	L	50
V	5	C	100
VI	6	D	500
VII	7	M	1000
VIII	8	MMIII	2003
IX	9	LXIII	63

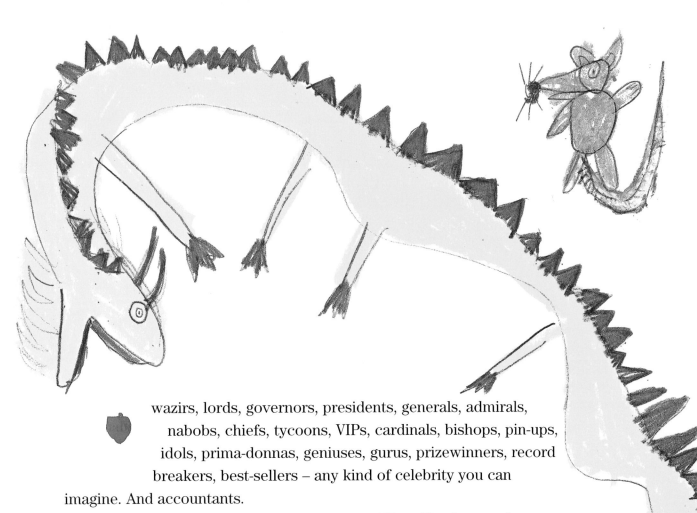

wazirs, lords, governors, presidents, generals, admirals, nabobs, chiefs, tycoons, VIPs, cardinals, bishops, pin-ups, idols, prima-donnas, geniuses, gurus, prizewinners, record breakers, best-sellers – any kind of celebrity you can imagine. And accountants.

Where was I? Oh, yes. Dragon, pool. Right. When Xiaolong woke up, he was starving ravenous hungry. He climbed out of the pool and stretched himself to quarter size, which is about three times as long as you are tall. He shook himself, flicked the water off his tail, and sniffed in a great snuff of air, searching for anything that smelled like food.

Dragon food isn't the same as human food or mouse food. You eat crisps and chocolate and chips and broccoli; we mice eat everything you eat plus stuff you don't, like glue and paper and soap and cardboard, and caterpillars and fly larvae and almost anything crunchy or squishy. Oh no – just thinking about it... I'm starving now!

Anyway – dragons. Chinese dragons eat birds and fish and lychees.

Xiaolong's favourite grub is jellyfish for starters and seagull for afters, which is lucky because there's loads and loads of them round here.

So anyway – Xiaolong was on the sniff for his tea, and he followed his nose to a hole in the wall. He shoved his head through and saw it was like a chimney that went up and up and up and up to a tiny patch of sky miles above him. And down that chimney wafted the smell of fresh seagull.

Xiaolong snorted an excited dragon snort, and there was a terrible squeak and some scrabbling and a small and furry thing fell on his nose. Xiaolong whipped his head out of the chimney, shook his head and something grey flew off. The grey something landed upside down in a puddle and lay still. Xiaolong prodded it with one claw and the grey something opened its eyes, turned itself over, saw the dragon, squeaked and tried to run off, but running is difficult when you're pinned down by a dragon's four claws.

'Eeeeeeek!' squeaked the something, which you've probably guessed was my brave ancestor, the First George. 'Eeeeeow!' he yelled. And then something amazing happened. George started to shout 'Shove off, you big bully!' but a claw tip caught his bottom and he said 'OW!!!' instead. And that sounded like: 'SH...OW!' Which did the trick. Xiaolong thought the creature had called his name and that was so magical to a lost and hungry dragon that he let go of George and said hello in Mandarin. Which sounded something like: '*Nin hao. Xing hui xing hui; wu ren jing pei.*'

That means: 'Hello, sir. I am most honoured to meet you; boundless respect and admiration.'

That might sound a bit posh for saying hello to a mouse, but Chinese dragons are very grand. More royal than kings, more imperial than emperors. They're celestial beings, so 'hello' doesn't do it for dragons.

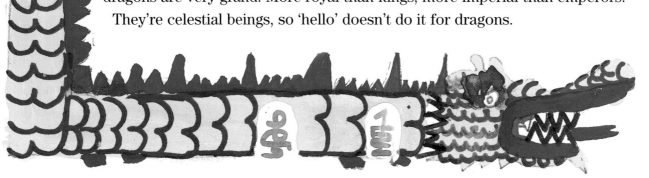

Anyway, George was dead impressed and didn't scarper, which was pretty brave. 'All right, mate?' said George, in a bit of a squeak because he was brave as a lion but even a lion might be a bit nervous around a dragon as big as a Number 27 bus. 'Don't know what you said there, la, but the same to you and welcome to Liverpool, mate.'

Then a magic thing happened, because dragons are a bit magic. Xiaolong shut his eyes tight. There was a rumble and a whoosh from somewhere inside him, and he opened his eyes, which gleamed blue like sapphires, and he took a deep breath... and in a mousy Scouse squeak, said: 'Fancy a bevvy, mate?'

George was so shocked he fell over. 'H-how did you do that?' he said.

Xiaolong looked really smug and said – still in the Scouse squeak: 'How can I explain. It's like an instant language school. I can access the linguistic centres in your cerebrum...'

'Er, hang on, mate. The what centres in my where?'

'The parts of your brain where you think about what you say,' said Xiaolong.

'Oh, right. You hungry?'

Xiaolong's tail lashed and there was a rumble from somewhere down his belly. So George climbed on Xiaolong's head; the dragon clambered into the chimney and with a scraping of claws on brick, whisked 38 metres up the shaft. Pop! his head shot out of the chimney like a chimney-sweep's brush.

It was still daylight, so George advised Xiaolong to grow small, even though they were up on the roof. 'No point in worrying people, is there?' he said. 'You never know who's looking.'

So Xiaolong squeezed down to the size of a sausage dog and stole three eggs from a seagull's nest. He'd have to wait till dark to grow big enough to bag a bird. Seagulls are bigger than sausage dogs and vicious feathery mouse-murdering thugs.

Chapter 4

Xiaolong got used to life in the Hall, with George to keep him out of trouble and away from human eyes. There was still another four years to go before the Hall was completely finished, so Xiaolong had to dodge workmen making a nuisance of themselves in the basement and mucking about on the roof. Xiaolong was forever changing size and even changing shape to avoid being noticed. Even a tiny Chinese dragon is a startling sight.

He was a bit gorgeous, even then, before he reached his 33rd birthday (when he grew into his third stage as a horned dragon). Xiaolong is a yellow dragon, which he says is the most specialest best colour to be. Actually he is more gold than yellow, specially when the sun makes his scales gleam. He's got a great big blonde mane like a lion, but clean and shiny. He's got long trailing whiskers that are azure blue (*azure* is another delicious word I ate from that dictionary) like a summer sky; same colour as the spines down his back, the tip of his tail and his toes. You wouldn't lose him in a crowd.

My dad George LXII told me: 'He's got this strange bump on his forehead which he says tingles till he wants to scream sometimes, but he can't remember what it's for. He thinks he banged his head when he fell into the ship in Shanghai because there are things he thinks he's forgotten, except he can't remember what it is he's forgotten, so he's not sure.'

Xiaolong and George were up on the roof one evening about a week after he arrived at the Hall; Xiaolong was munching on a seagull he'd caught, and George had an apple core he'd liberated from the kitchens. Xiaolong loved the roof, especially at night when he could stretch out full size and watch the city, listen to the ships' hooters and bells on the river, and stare out to sea.

Xiaolong was muttering something in Mandarin. George stopped eating and stared at him. 'What?' he said.

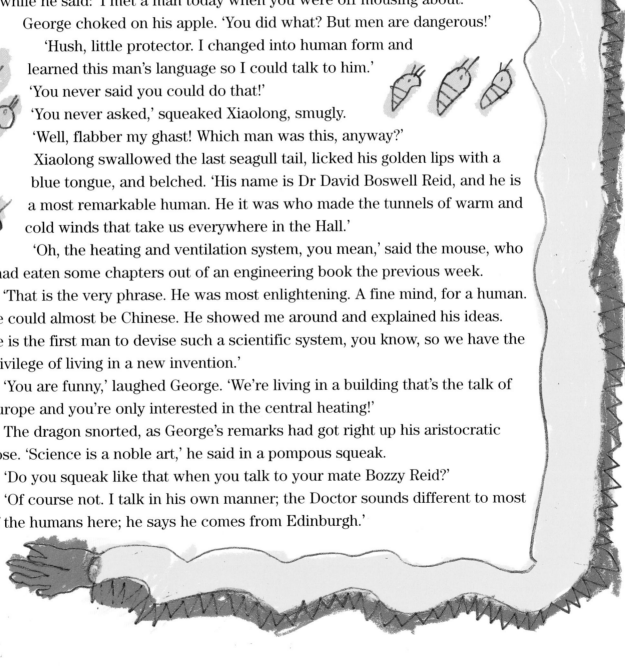

'A dragon which swims in shallow water will be attacked by shrimps,' Xiaolong translated. George was still lost. 'What *are* you going on about?'

Xiaolong gave him a funny look but said nothing. Chinese dragons are not only very old but very mystical, and not always helpful. But after a while he said: 'I met a man today when you were off mousing about.'

George choked on his apple. 'You did what? But men are dangerous!'

'Hush, little protector. I changed into human form and learned this man's language so I could talk to him.'

'You never said you could do that!'

'You never asked,' squeaked Xiaolong, smugly.

'Well, flabber my ghast! Which man was this, anyway?'

Xiaolong swallowed the last seagull tail, licked his golden lips with a blue tongue, and belched. 'His name is Dr David Boswell Reid, and he is a most remarkable human. He it was who made the tunnels of warm and cold winds that take us everywhere in the Hall.'

'Oh, the heating and ventilation system, you mean,' said the mouse, who had eaten some chapters out of an engineering book the previous week.

'That is the very phrase. He was most enlightening. A fine mind, for a human. He could almost be Chinese. He showed me around and explained his ideas. He is the first man to devise such a scientific system, you know, so we have the privilege of living in a new invention.'

'You are funny,' laughed George. 'We're living in a building that's the talk of Europe and you're only interested in the central heating!'

The dragon snorted, as George's remarks had got right up his aristocratic nose. 'Science is a noble art,' he said in a pompous squeak.

'Do you squeak like that when you talk to your mate Bozzy Reid?'

'Of course not. I talk in his own manner; the Doctor sounds different to most of the humans here; he says he comes from Edinburgh.'

'Oh, yeh. A Scotsman, then. They do talk peculiar up there, it's true. They go rrrrrrrrrrr like they're growling and kkhhhhhhhh like they're going to be sick. Weird, if you ask me. But I must say you've got the accent off pat.'

There was a silence while George finished his apple. Xiaolong drank in the sight of carriage lanterns bobbing through the fog below, and the muffled sounds of horses' hooves on the cobbles.

'I must speak to the human Cockerell.'

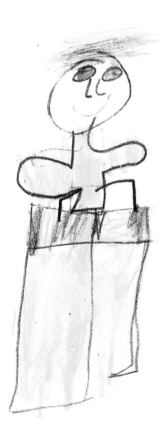

'The human cockerel?' said George, thinking of a big chicken in a frock coat.

'Sir Charles Cockerell, the architect. He can tell me the true purpose of this place. I believe him to be the master of the enterprise.'

George sighed. 'I wish you'd go back to my language and forget all those posh words you got from Bozzy. You'll do my head in. Anyway, he's not. Charlie – he's not the boss. Well, I suppose he is now since poor Harvey died a few years ago. He was only 33 – same age as you and me, mate. That's too young.'

Xiaolong cocked his head to one side. 'Harvey?'

'Harvey Lonsdale Elmes, the bloke who designed this whole place. 'Brilliant, he was. I read all about him in a magazine I was having for pudding. Died of consumption.'

'He was consumed? What creature would eat a human?' asked the dragon.

20

'No, mate – *consumption*. It's a human disease. Coughing up blood till you snuff it. Horrible. They reckon that building the Hall did for poor Harvey. Too much hard work. And travelling up and down to London. Very stressful.'

'So this Cockerell – he is merely an underling?'

George sneezed. 'Oh, no! He's a big architect and Harvey's mate. He's taking over to get the Hall finished. Well, you can see how much there's still to do. The Courts aren't ready yet and they're supposed to be open soon.'

'Ah yes, the courts. This is what I don't understand,' said Xiaolong. 'These courts are for process of law, yes?' George nodded. 'So why is there to be a place for music and dancing between the courts? Is the law an entertainment in this country? Or is the music to soothe the prisoners?'

George gasped. 'No! The law is very serious, and not funny at all. Especially if you're being hanged in the morning.'

The dragon raised a blue eyebrow, but said nothing. George continued: 'Right. First off, all the big-wigs in Liverpool decided they needed a new concert hall for all the music festivals they had planned. So they got Harvey to design one. Then they wanted another new building for law courts because Liverpool was getting so big and rich and lots of extra criminals were getting caught. And Harvey designed that building too. Then the big-wigs realised it was daft to build two expensive buildings so they got Harvey to squish the two together, somehow. Which is how we got this place.

'It's going to have two assize courts and a massive concert hall and another little concert room and there's going to be all sorts happening here. Dinners – yum yum – and fairs and charity balls and bazaars and plays and rallies and dances and exhibitions and...'

'Ah, yes, Justice, Charity, Culture. Very good,' said the dragon, who had heard enough of civic plans and wanted to have a snooze.

The two friends made their way back down from roof to basement, and while Xiaolong squeezed himself down into his pool at the base of the sandstone outcrop, George went off to see to his mouse family.

They'd never meet again. While Xiaolong was sleeping, George met a cat in the kitchens, and came off worse. If that's what you'd call being eaten after half an hour of torture. Us mice don't have it easy, you know.

Chapter 5

When Xiaolong woke, he saw a row of little mousy faces looking down at him from the top of the rock. The biggest, seeing the dragon wake and uncurl himself from the pool, cleared his throat and stepped forward. 'Hello, Mr Xiaolong, your Excellency,' he said in a shaky voice.

Xiaolong said: '*Ni hao*, George. You well?'

The mouse looked very nervous. 'Er, I'm not George, your Celestialness. He was my Dad but he died a year ago. I'm Gregory and I'm your protector now.'

The dragon frowned. 'Don't be silly, George. I've only been asleep for a day. Stop messing about. Is this your family? Very good. Come, it's time for dinner.'

And that was it. Gregory, George's eldest son, became George II and began the tradition that passed from father mouse to son mouse all the way down to me, George LXIII, or Gezza, as you know me.

The problem was this thing of dragon time and mouse time. Dragons live 900 times longer than mice, so a year to a mouse is only about eight hours to a dragon, and three weeks to you humans. You can see why it's so confusing.

Anyway, Xiaolong and a string of Georges were pretty happy in the Hall, staying out of human sight – unless Xiaolong wanted to chat to people he liked the look of, when he turned into a human with a shock of blond hair, golden skin, very blue almond-shaped eyes and rather strange clothes.

The dragon in his human disguise had long chats about literature with the famous author Charles Dickens, sitting in his dressing room before Dickens gave readings from his novels in the small concert room.

Xiaolong was also completely smitten with the great organ built by Father Willis in the Hall, and spent long hours nosing about among the 7,737 pipes and down in the bellows room. In human disguise he would sit and watch the amazing Mr William T Best play the world's biggest musical instrument.

Mr William who, like most great organists, was completely bonkers, took a liking to the strange looking fellow in the gold and blue suit and agreed to give him lessons. Xiaolong learned very quickly, of course, and played the organ for George in the early hours of the night when no-one was around. George would rather have snacked on the chewy bits inside the organ mechanism, but Xiaolong wouldn't let him.

One of their favourite games was playing slide on the floor of the big hall. You should see it – it's a huge mosaic like in a Roman palace – 30,000 little tiles which make up swirly patterns. The hall is big enough for Xiaolong to be at full size and still have room to whoosh about with the mouse clinging on to his whiskers. It was even better when the wooden dance floor was down...

What most upset Xiaolong was the court stuff – justice in Victorian times was a bit rough if you came from the wrong end of town. Xiaolong and George would often creep down at night to the cells where prisoners were kept during their trials; sometimes they'd hear a man weeping, and then Xiaolong would sing a dragon song to send the prisoner to sleep and dream of mountain lakes and cherry blossom and nesting swallows.

Sometimes Xiaolong would squeeze himself under the door, small as a silkworm, then take on his human disguise to talk to the man or woman in the cell. The prisoner usually thought he was an angel, but once or twice they screamed and screamed because they were convinced he was the Devil come for their souls...

One of the strangest women Xiaolong met was Florence Maybrick, who had killed her husband James in 1889. 'She thought she was going mad when she saw me,' he said to George XVI. 'But she talked anyway. Helped her, she said, to talk it through, even if I was only a dream.

'She whispered to me that she'd found out that her husband was an evil man who had to be stopped. She said: "Jack was insane, a demon unleashed." She said, George, that he had killed five women in London, but no-one would ever believe it. So she had no choice, she said. Poor young woman. I don't believe we will ever know the truth of it.'

Xiaolong spent several nights in 1931 talking to one man on trial for murder. Herbert Wallace, his name was, supposed to have killed his wife Julia.

'The poor man is bemused and in despair,' the dragon told George XXVII after the first night. 'Not only has he lost his beloved wife, but could lose his own life to the hangman. I believe he is innocent, but he has no explanation for what happened and for an alibi can only offer the name of a mysterious caller, Mr Qualtrough. I fear for him, George.'

When a young Chinese lad was sentenced to hang for stealing from a local merchant,

Xiaolong got really, really angry.

'The judge is a bigoted bully,' seethed the dragon. 'There was no evidence. The boy is innocent. I want to give that betrayer of Justice a taste of bitter medicine.'

So Xiaolong waited till the next time this judge turned up in Court No 1. Over the main doors to Court No 1 is a passageway where you can see down into the court, but the only place you can see the passageway clearly is from the judge's chair. 'I waited up there, hiding until the afternoon session,' Xiaolong told George. 'I chose my moment, stretched to full size and got the judge's attention with a little dragon trick. The dreadful man looked up to where I was and shrieked in horror to see a raging dragon come to send him to Hell.'

Xiaolong laughed; George shuddered.

'The judge wouldn't stop screaming. The Court was in uproar; when people looked to see what had so affected the judge, there was nothing there.'

'But you could have been seen!' George was horrified. 'What if someone had found you? They'd have killed you!'

'But they didn't,' said the dragon calmly. 'The judge was dragged out, still shrieking, and I gather he has completely lost his wits and has now been incarcerated in a lunatic asylum. *Ding gua gua.*'

Xiaolong gave a thumbs-up sign, but his eyes were cold.

A dragon's anger is no joke, believe me – you don't ever want to find out.

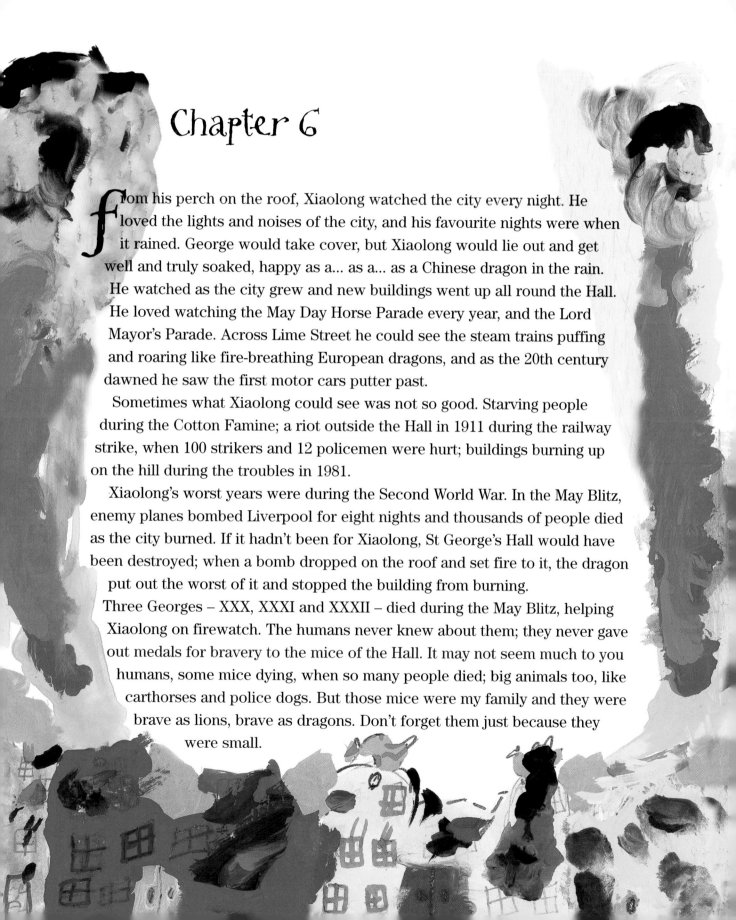

Chapter 6

From his perch on the roof, Xiaolong watched the city every night. He loved the lights and noises of the city, and his favourite nights were when it rained. George would take cover, but Xiaolong would lie out and get well and truly soaked, happy as a... as a... as a Chinese dragon in the rain. He watched as the city grew and new buildings went up all round the Hall. He loved watching the May Day Horse Parade every year, and the Lord Mayor's Parade. Across Lime Street he could see the steam trains puffing and roaring like fire-breathing European dragons, and as the 20th century dawned he saw the first motor cars putter past.

Sometimes what Xiaolong could see was not so good. Starving people during the Cotton Famine; a riot outside the Hall in 1911 during the railway strike, when 100 strikers and 12 policemen were hurt; buildings burning up on the hill during the troubles in 1981.

Xiaolong's worst years were during the Second World War. In the May Blitz, enemy planes bombed Liverpool for eight nights and thousands of people died as the city burned. If it hadn't been for Xiaolong, St George's Hall would have been destroyed; when a bomb dropped on the roof and set fire to it, the dragon put out the worst of it and stopped the building from burning.

Three Georges – XXX, XXXI and XXXII – died during the May Blitz, helping Xiaolong on firewatch. The humans never knew about them; they never gave out medals for bravery to the mice of the Hall. It may not seem much to you humans, some mice dying, when so many people died; big animals too, like carthorses and police dogs. But those mice were my family and they were brave as lions, brave as dragons. Don't forget them just because they were small.

Chapter 7

Xiaolong had lived in St George's Hall for just over 100 years by the start of the 1960s, and he was beginning to settle down (don't forget that 100 human years is only about 18 months to a dragon) and enjoy life in Liverpool. He had his mouse friends and he was meeting people, and he loved watching from the roof as the city changed and buildings came and went.

One of Xiaolong's favourite buildings is what we mice called the Doughnut on a Stick. Its real name is St John's Beacon, and it's actually the chimney for St John's Market with a radio station on top. You can see forever from up there – I went up there once with my cousin Wacker Jack when I was very young. It's cool! Xiaolong wants to go up there; he thinks he'll see China. You can see Wales, but isn't China a bit further away than that?

Oh, by the way, did I tell you Xiaolong wrote a pop song? There was this time – 1963, I think? – Xiaolong was in the small concert room, singing to George and some other mice, and Jinx the cat. Xiaolong was singing his favourite Chinese dragon song. It was about a dragon called Lu Chi who was famous for his flashing eyes. I can't remember what it was called, but the chorus went: 'Lu Chi's in the skies with diamond eyes'.

Anyway, at the end of the song someone started clapping. All the mice ran away and hid, and Xiaolong looked a bit startled. Two humans appeared, still clapping. They didn't seem at all surprised that Xiaolong was a dragon.

'That was fab, la,' said one. 'Amazing, in fact. I didn't know dragons could sing. My name's John, by the way, and this is my mate Paul.'

Xiaolong changed into his blue-eyed human shape, bowed to the two young men and introduced himself.

'That's cool, man. What a great outfit,' said Paul. Xiaolong bowed again.

'What was that song, mate?' asked John.

'Only we're in a band, you see, and we'd like to sing it. What was it – Lucy in the sky..?'

'Lu Chi in the skies with diamond eyes,' said Xiaolong.

'Could we sing it?' said Paul. 'We'd pay you, like.'

Xiaolong bowed again. 'I have no use for money. You are most welcome,' he said. And a few years later a song called 'Lucy in the sky with diamonds' was a big hit for the Beatles and not many people understood what the words meant, but that was OK because it was a great song anyway.

Chapter 8

It's no good – I can't wait any longer –
I've GOT to tell you what happened to
me and Xiaolong. It was amazing... It's like
a fairy tale when I look back on the day that the dragon stopped squeaking.

It was about a year after I took over from my Dad that Xiaolong started
getting these horrible headaches. Xiaolong had killed my Dad, by the way –
knocked him flying off the roof with his tail. He didn't mean to, but he's killed
a few Georges. Some got squashed underfoot, a couple got eaten, and one got
rolled on. He never realises, because he's never got his head round the fact that
there's more than one mouse. He'd be really really upset if he knew.

Poor old Xiaolong suffered a lot when my Dad went off the edge – Xiaolong
didn't have the courage to leap off after him. He didn't think he could fly, you
see, and he felt so guilty that he cried. When he saw me he danced, he was so
happy – he thought my Dad had survived somehow and come back. But it was
me, of course. I didn't tell him – he wouldn't have believed me anyway. But he
couldn't get over not flying to my Dad's rescue.

That's when he started getting nightmares and headaches.

'I dream everything is noise and thunder and blackness and screaming,' he'd
say in the saddest voice you can imagine. 'And there are voices in my head.'

This went on for days. I was getting really scared for him. His scales were
fading to a sickly yellow and his eyes had gone a dull grey colour. I asked him
what the voices said. 'I can't really explain, George. They are calling me; they
tell me to fly, and wake them up,' he said. 'The wind blows and the grass bends.'
I didn't have a clue what he was talking about.

After five days of this Xiaolong was going mad; he hadn't eaten for two days,
which shows how bad he was. But the seagulls were all going mad, too. They're

30

always noisy, but they were screaming their heads off and flying like lunatics.

Then that night I met a rat. There are no rats in the Hall – they all left when Xiaolong arrived. This one said his name was Hartley and he lived near the Albert Dock. 'I come with a warning,' he said in his harsh ratty voice. 'The Liver Birds say there is danger. The sea will swallow the city.'

I took Hartley up to the roof, where Xiaolong lay exhausted and miserable. I made the river rat say everything again. Xiaolong asked: 'Liver Birds?'

'You've seen pictures of them all over the Hall,' I said. 'Over the doors and on the floor, and in the stained glass window above the organ.'

Hartley pointed west across the city to the Liver Building on the waterfront. Standing on the towers are the two Liver Birds, great green birds with their wings outstretched. 'They're the guardians of Liverpool,' said the river rat.

Xialong nodded. 'We must ask the Liver Birds more,' he said. We waited till daybreak, when birds wake up. Xiaolong called to the seagulls when they began to fly overhead, but as he usually ate them, the seagulls made rude noises at him. A starling perched on the flagpole had been eavesdropping and chirped up: 'I'll do it, mate. I don't mind.' And she flapped off towards the river.

Xiaolong and I waited on the roof for ages and ages. It felt like years, but it was probably only a little while before the starling came back, landing with a flurry of shiny green-black feathers.

'OK, well, it's complicated,' said the starling. 'The Liver Birds got this from some dolphins who live near the gas rigs out in Liverpool Bay. They use long words like 'tectonics', 'lithosphere' and 'hydrostatic pressure' because they're very clever, but I had to get the Liver Birds to explain it to me.'

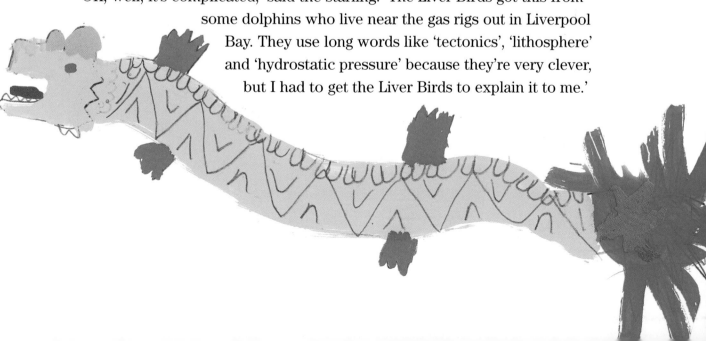

Xiaolong shifted impatiently. 'Tell me, bird. Get on with it,' he said.

'My name's Kelly, if you don't mind,' said the bird sternly. Xiaolong raised one eyebrow and I giggled at a starling ticking off a celestial dragon.

Kelly continued: 'Well, it's all about big gas bubbles under the sea bed. Methane, the gas is called, which is the scientific word for farts. Anyway, I don't really understand but the dolphins say that these gas bubbles build up in the sea bed and they're going to explode under the sea like a volcano. And there's something called a fault line out in the bay, which is why we sometimes get little earthquakes here and the big fart volcano will make a huge earthquake underwater. And that will make a GIANT wave called a tsunami 20 metres high which will rush in and hit Liverpool and all the people and mice and dogs and rats and cats and beetles and nesting birds and all sorts will be drowned *dead*...'

The starling gasped for breath. '... unless you stop it,' she said to Xiaolong.

'How?' the dragon asked. 'How can I help when I'm stuck here?'

Then Xiaolong heard the voices again. 'Fly, little dragon, fly. Don't think, fly.' But Xiaolong was frightened.

He stepped on to the parapet and looked down at the city. How could he fly? He had no wings. He stumbled back from the edge to safety. But the voices kept on at him, getting louder and louder inside his head.

'Fight against furious waves – take a chance and face the storm! Fly to us, little brother, fly!'

Suddenly Xiaolong looked very serious and sad, and bent his head down to me. He whispered: 'This is the single moment of a thousand years. We are sworn brothers, little George – we will meet again, in this life or the next.'

And before I could say a word, Xiaolong stepped on to the parapet and leapt into the air...

... and he FLEW! He flew like the celestial dragon he was, leaping through the clouds, twisting and coiling in the sky, his golden scales glinting in the sun, his sapphire eyes flashing.

Then I fell over in amazement as Xiaolong the dragon roared a great dragon roar. Not a mousy squeak, not a rumble, but a roar that made the air tremble and the ground quake. It seemed like everything stopped, like the world came to a halt for a moment. My heart was thumping and I could hardly breathe. Then I was dancing and leaping on the roof of the Hall, yelling and squeaking at the top of my voice: 'Go, Xiaolong, go! Eeeiiiaaaoo!!! Yiaaaoooeee!!!'

Then everything speeded up and everything seemed to happen in a flash. Xiaolong followed the sound of the voices and flew

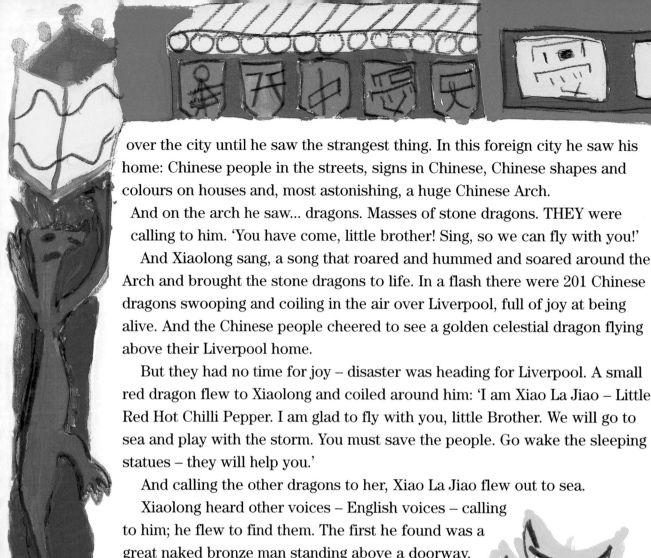

over the city until he saw the strangest thing. In this foreign city he saw his home: Chinese people in the streets, signs in Chinese, Chinese shapes and colours on houses and, most astonishing, a huge Chinese Arch.

And on the arch he saw... dragons. Masses of stone dragons. THEY were calling to him. 'You have come, little brother! Sing, so we can fly with you!'

And Xiaolong sang, a song that roared and hummed and soared around the Arch and brought the stone dragons to life. In a flash there were 201 Chinese dragons swooping and coiling in the air over Liverpool, full of joy at being alive. And the Chinese people cheered to see a golden celestial dragon flying above their Liverpool home.

But they had no time for joy – disaster was heading for Liverpool. A small red dragon flew to Xiaolong and coiled around him: 'I am Xiao La Jiao – Little Red Hot Chilli Pepper. I am glad to fly with you, little Brother. We will go to sea and play with the storm. You must save the people. Go wake the sleeping statues – they will help you.'

And calling the other dragons to her, Xiao La Jiao flew out to sea.

Xiaolong heard other voices – English voices – calling to him; he flew to find them. The first he found was a great naked bronze man standing above a doorway. Xiaolong swooped down to him and roared; the statue shivered and stood upright, waving at the dragon. 'My name's Dicky Lewis!' he shouted up to Xiaolong. 'What can I do to help?'

The dragon laughed: 'You'd better get some kecks on, la! Then start warning people not to go near the river – get them up the hill.'

And with a flick of his blue tail, Xiaolong flew on in his race against time.

Chapter 9

Below Xiaolong, on the streets, in cars, on buses and through windows, people were gawping up at the unbelievable sight of a 20 metre golden dragon flying just above them. Some of the people were terrified; their screams pierced Xiaolong like needles and he called down to them. 'Don't be frightened – I am your neighbour and will not hurt you. But there is a flood coming – you must get to safety!' But a Chinese dragon speaking English was more than some people could cope with and a few passed out in terror. Others panicked and ran, but most people were entranced by the glorious sight of Xiaolong in the sky, scales gleaming, eyes flashing like sapphires.

They called up: 'What can we do? Tell us what to do!' Xiaolong landed on a roof and called out: 'We must keep everyone away from the river. You are on high ground here, so stop anyone going down the hill. Can you do that?'

There was a great shout as hundreds of people cheered and promised to help. Xiaolong flew on. On St George's Plateau he woke up the statues of Queen Victoria, Prince Albert and their horses, and the four huge lions. To the lions Xiaolong roared: 'Down to the river, and save all the children! They can ride on your back – bring them up the hill to high ground.' The lions roared, shook their manes and raced off, down the hill towards the river.

Victoria and Albert didn't need telling. With a wave to Xiaolong, the young Queen and her prince consort wheeled their horses, galloped down to the Mersey Tunnel and thundered through, to the astonishment of car drivers and people on buses. When they got to the Birkenhead side they stopped all traffic from going into the tunnel and got the police moving (once the poor chaps got over the shock of being ordered about by royal statues).

Meanwhile, out in Liverpool Bay, the dragons were searching for signs of the underwater volcano. Xiao La Jiao, the fiery little red dragon, dived deep beneath the surface, following her nose till she found the deadly volcano simmering beneath the sea bed. She shot to the surface and leaped into the sky, calling to Xiaolong: 'It is boiling and bubbling! I don't think it will be long before it explodes – you must hurry, little brother – come to our aid. We are a flock of dragons without a head. We need you!'

Hearing his fiery red friend, Xiaolong flew even faster. He woke the soldiers on the King's Regiment Memorial and he woke up King George V and Queen Mary, who worked together quickly to stop the cars going into the tunnel from Liverpool. If the tsunami hit Liverpool, the Mersey Tunnel would be flooded and everyone in it drowned for sure. No-one dared argue with a king, a queen and the King's Regiment, and within a few minutes the tunnel was empty and under guard by the soldiers.

Victoria and Albert raced back through the tunnel, their horses' hooves echoing like thunder. 'Come on!' shouted Prince Albert to King George, 'we must alert the city council!'

King George and Queen Mary climbed on to the horses behind Albert and Victoria and the four cantered down the street. George and Mary jumped off at the council offices to find the fellow in charge while Victoria and Albert raced on to the Town Hall and the city councillors.

Xiaolong, by this time, had woken Minerva on top of the Town Hall dome, and Admiral Nelson nearby. Nelson, who didn't have any clothes on, grabbed a Union Jack flag and wrapped

himself in it like a sarong before leaping off his pedestal and running down towards the Pier Head to take command of a ship and run operations on the water.

Out at sea, the dragons were hovering around the undersea volcano. All at once they heard a noise that made their spines tingle – a terrible rumble so low the dragons didn't so much hear it as feel it rattling through their bones…

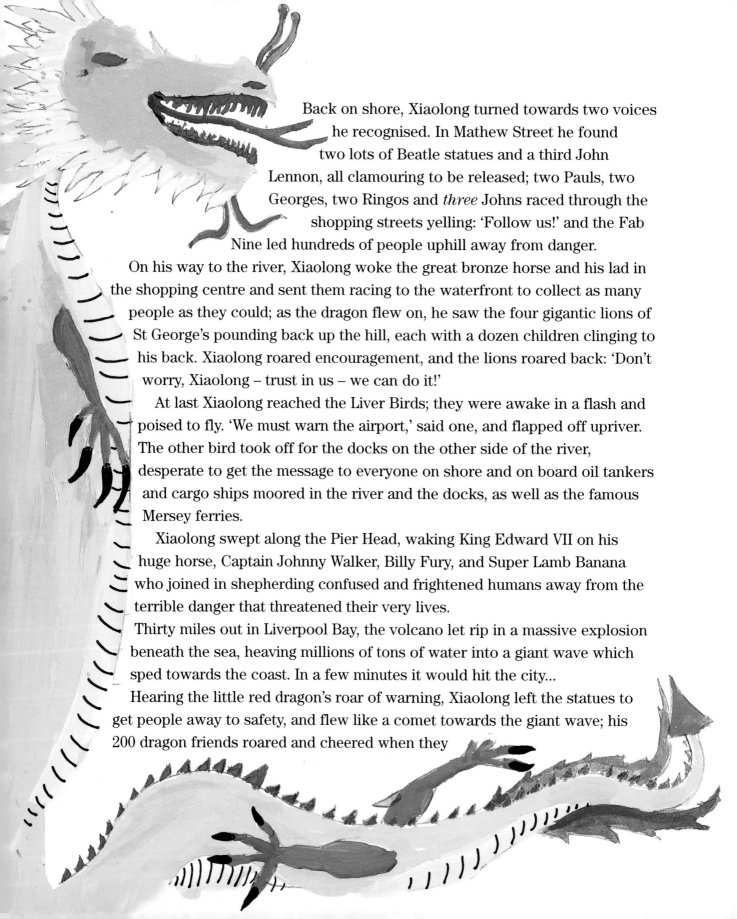

Back on shore, Xiaolong turned towards two voices he recognised. In Mathew Street he found two lots of Beatle statues and a third John Lennon, all clamouring to be released; two Pauls, two Georges, two Ringos and *three* Johns raced through the shopping streets yelling: 'Follow us!' and the Fab Nine led hundreds of people uphill away from danger.

On his way to the river, Xiaolong woke the great bronze horse and his lad in the shopping centre and sent them racing to the waterfront to collect as many people as they could; as the dragon flew on, he saw the four gigantic lions of St George's pounding back up the hill, each with a dozen children clinging to his back. Xiaolong roared encouragement, and the lions roared back: 'Don't worry, Xiaolong – trust in us – we can do it!'

At last Xiaolong reached the Liver Birds; they were awake in a flash and poised to fly. 'We must warn the airport,' said one, and flapped off upriver. The other bird took off for the docks on the other side of the river, desperate to get the message to everyone on shore and on board oil tankers and cargo ships moored in the river and the docks, as well as the famous Mersey ferries.

Xiaolong swept along the Pier Head, waking King Edward VII on his huge horse, Captain Johnny Walker, Billy Fury, and Super Lamb Banana who joined in shepherding confused and frightened humans away from the terrible danger that threatened their very lives.

Thirty miles out in Liverpool Bay, the volcano let rip in a massive explosion beneath the sea, heaving millions of tons of water into a giant wave which sped towards the coast. In a few minutes it would hit the city...

Hearing the little red dragon's roar of warning, Xiaolong left the statues to get people away to safety, and flew like a comet towards the giant wave; his 200 dragon friends roared and cheered when they

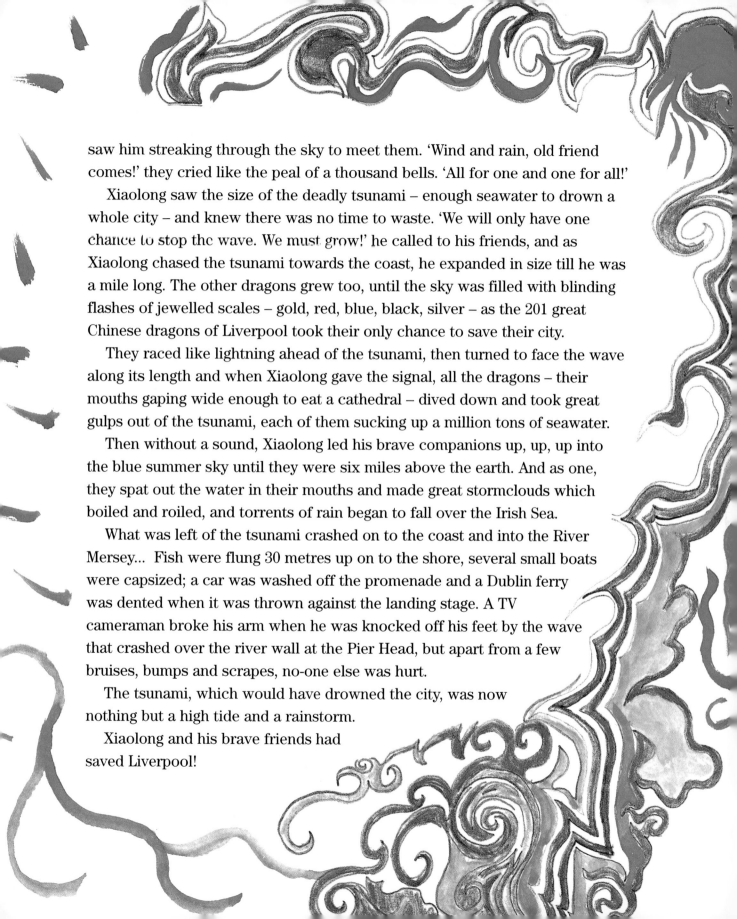

saw him streaking through the sky to meet them. 'Wind and rain, old friend comes!' they cried like the peal of a thousand bells. 'All for one and one for all!'

Xiaolong saw the size of the deadly tsunami – enough seawater to drown a whole city – and knew there was no time to waste. 'We will only have one chance to stop the wave. We must grow!' he called to his friends, and as Xiaolong chased the tsunami towards the coast, he expanded in size till he was a mile long. The other dragons grew too, until the sky was filled with blinding flashes of jewelled scales – gold, red, blue, black, silver – as the 201 great Chinese dragons of Liverpool took their only chance to save their city.

They raced like lightning ahead of the tsunami, then turned to face the wave along its length and when Xiaolong gave the signal, all the dragons – their mouths gaping wide enough to eat a cathedral – dived down and took great gulps out of the tsunami, each of them sucking up a million tons of seawater.

Then without a sound, Xiaolong led his brave companions up, up, up into the blue summer sky until they were six miles above the earth. And as one, they spat out the water in their mouths and made great stormclouds which boiled and roiled, and torrents of rain began to fall over the Irish Sea.

What was left of the tsunami crashed on to the coast and into the River Mersey... Fish were flung 30 metres up on to the shore, several small boats were capsized; a car was washed off the promenade and a Dublin ferry was dented when it was thrown against the landing stage. A TV cameraman broke his arm when he was knocked off his feet by the wave that crashed over the river wall at the Pier Head, but apart from a few bruises, bumps and scrapes, no-one else was hurt.

The tsunami, which would have drowned the city, was now nothing but a high tide and a rainstorm.

Xiaolong and his brave friends had saved Liverpool!

Chapter 10

When Xiaolong, his little fiery friend Xiao La Jiao, and the other 199 dragons flew down to the Pier Head, they heard whistling and cheering and clapping, horns hooting, bells pealing, sirens and klaxons. The whole city was celebrating and cheering their fantastic rescuers.

All the statues – Nelson, Queen Victoria, the Beatles, Dicky Lewis, the lions, everyone – crowded on to the lawns; people were hanging out of every window in the buildings along the waterfront, and waving from the roof, and flocking down from the city. Soon you couldn't budge for the heaving mass of happy, amazed people crowding round their heroes.

How do I know? Because I, Gezza the Scouse Mouse, was right there! Remember Kelly the starling? Well, she carried me all the way from the roof of St George's Hall, swooping over the city (what a way to travel!!) and landed me right on top of Xiaolong's head. It was the proudest moment of my life.

The Lord Mayor made a speech, and everyone cheered. Then the Council Leader made a speech, and everyone cheered again. Then everyone had had enough of speeches and wanted a party.

That was the BIGGEST and LONGEST and NOISIEST and HAPPIEST party Liverpool has ever seen. The kings and queens danced with the soldiers and the children danced with the Beatles. Nelson and Dicky Lewis were dancing with the Lord Mayor. The horses, lions and Super Lamb Banana were prancing about like lunatics, and the Liver Birds were swooping around with the dragons.

After a while, Xiaolong felt a bit tired – it had been a busy day, after all. So he became the size of a silkworm, and he and I sneaked off quietly and hitched a ride with a Liver Bird back to St George's Hall. While Liverpool partied till dawn, me and my best mate Xiaolong went home for a kip.

The End

St George's Hall

St George's Hall is one of the finest neo-classical buildings in Europe. Queen Victoria, on a visit to Liverpool in 1851, described St Georges Hall as 'worthy of ancient Athens'. Completed in 1854, it was designed by a young architect, Harvey Lonsdale Elmes as law courts and as a venue for music festivals, dinners, concerts, fairs, exhibitions and much more.

The splendid Great Hall, with its vaulted ceiling, houses the magnificent Willis organ – one of the largest organs in the country, and one of the finest concert organs in the world. The Hall's Minton tiled floor consists of upwards of 30,000 tiles, laid in 1852 at a cost of £2000. Today it is beyond price, because the tiled floor is the largest of its kind, anywhere in the world.

The Small Concert Hall was opened to the public in 1856. Charles Dickens gave many of his readings from here in the 1860s. He became so popular that on 10th April 1869 a grand banquet was given in his honour by the Corporation before he sailed to America.

St George's Hall's courts closed in 1984, but many famous murder trials were heard in the Crown Court, such as Mrs Maybrick in 1889, the Wallace case in 1929 and, in 1950, the Cameo Murders. During his short career in the law, WS Gilbert appeared several times as a barrister in the Civil Court before teaming up with Sir Arthur Sullivan to become famous for their much-loved operettas.

Since the courts closed, much of the building has deteriorated and significant spaces are unusable. Liverpool City Council is now leading an £18 million project to restore the hall as an exciting attraction for arts, heritage and business use. To complete this project we need to raise £1.5 million, and a number of fundraising initiatives have been launched. We are very pleased that the Duke of Westminster has agreed to be the principal patron of the Appeal. By buying this book you are contributing to our goal and we hope that we can now count on your further support.

'One of the greatest public buildings of the last 200 years,
which sits in the very centre of one of Europe's finest cities'
HRH Prince Charles, November 1990

All proceeds from the sale of this book will go
towards the restoration of the Hall and the organ

Garlic Press

Garlic Press Publishing is a Liverpool-based company that specialises in beautiful books about this splendid city. Garlic's first book, *Liverpool; the first 1,000 years*, sold out in 40 days when it was published in 2001, and has become the standard reference book on the city. It was part of the city's arsenal in the bid to win Capital of Culture status and has even been quoted in a House of Lords debate. Every book since has added to the weight of evidence demonstrating Liverpool's world class, be it in sport, music, architecture, innovation, art, medicine, learning, comedy... and on it goes.

For every 12 months leading up to Liverpool's year as Capital of Culture in 2008, there will be a long list of publications for Garlic Press to produce – culminating in a barnstorming Birthday Book for Liverpool's 800th anniversary.

Previous books include: • Liverpool: the first 1,000 years • The Christmas Day Liverpool Quiz Book •
• SHEDKM - first five years in Liverpool • The Grand National Quiz Book • Cross the Mersey •
• MMLL: Mike McCartney's Liverpool Life

Arabella McIntyre-Brown

Born and educated in West Sussex, she lived in London for 11 years before falling in love with Liverpool in 1988.
In London she worked for the RSC, ENO, the Arts Council, and at Camden Lock, amongst others.
In Liverpool she became a journalist and was editor of business magazines for over 12 years. She now writes books about Liverpool for Garlic Press, and lives between Sefton Park and the River Mersey.

Thanks

We are grateful to everyone who helped us get the book from an idea to publication:
Graham Boxer, Hazel Russell, Karen Gallagher and the team at St George's Hall.
MGL for their kind support.
Liverpool City Council and St George's Hall Trustees for their support throughout.
The art competition judges Steve Baker, Stephen Broadbent, Paige Earlham, Ken Martin and Joe Riley. The competition sponsors Davis Langdon & Everest, Purcell Miller Tritton, Schal, and Mowlem. Banks Road Primary for the help with the competition launch.
Rennies Art Shop for their help.
Ken Martin (again) for the exhibition of dragons at his View Two Gallery.
Rob Shorland-Ball for sparking off the whole project.
Niall McQuistan for oil industry expertise; Sean McQuistan for oceanography advice.
Charlotte Pepper for Mandarin greetings.
Sam Armstrong, Brittany and Melissa Fearon, Sarah Garrett, Stefanie and Alexander Gorman, Dhugal and Finlay McQuistan, and Henry Woodland, for candid criticism.
Parents and teachers of the illustrators.
As always, our gratitude to a splendid team of colleagues and friends whose talent, expertise and enthusiasm make our job so much easier.

Notes

p25 Mrs Florence Maybrick was accused of murdering her English husband James. They lived at Battlecrease House in Aigburth (Liverpool 17), where diaries were discovered in 1991 that made many people believe that James Maybrick was the serial killer Jack the Ripper.

p32 Mud **volcanoes** are quite common in the oil fields of Azerbaijan, but there is no risk of methane gas building up in Liverpool Bay. There have been little tiny earthquakes felt in Liverpool, but they are hardly strong enough to wake you up. **Tsunamis** happen quite a lot in warmer parts of the world, but there has never been one in Britain and there is never likely to be one in the future.

The statues

There are dozens of statues in Liverpool, but Xiaolong did not have time to wake them all up. Here's where you'll find the ones he did get to help:

A: Victoria and Albert and **B: the four lions**: on St George's Plateau, outside St George's Hall.

C: The Great Escape: the 12-foot high horse and the boy trying to stop him escaping is at the top of Church Street, near Clayton Square.

D: The Beatles: there are three sculpture groups of the Beatles in Mathew Street; one in Cavern Walks, one above the Beatles Shop and one high on the wall opposite the Cavern. This, though, is the Beatles as babes in arms, so Xiaolong did not disturb them. The statue of John Lennon is leaning against a doorway.

E: Dicky Lewis: the statue by Jacob Epstein is really called 'Liverpool Resurgent', but got its cheeky nickname because it's a nude, and stands over the doorway to Lewis's store opposite the Adelphi Hotel.

F: Admiral Nelson: the Nelson Memorial is on Exchange Flags.

G: Minerva: she sits on the dome of the Town Hall in Castle Street.

H: King George V and Queen Mary: they stand either side of the Liverpool entrance to the Queensway (Birkenhead) Tunnel.

I: The Liver Birds: on the Royal Liver Building, Pier Head.

J: Super Lamb Banana: in Wapping, outside JP Lamb the chandlers.

Edward VII, and Captain Johnny Walker: at the Pier Head.

Billy Fury: at the Museum of Liverpool Life, near Albert Dock.

The King's Regiment Memorial: in St John's Gardens, to the west of St George's Hall.

The illustrators

The competition to find the illustrators for this book was launched at Chinese New Year, in February 2003. There were 1,107 entries from schools on Merseyside, with ages ranging from five to 17. On St George's Day, 23rd April 2003, the judges chose the images they liked best without looking at entry forms, so their decisions were made purely on merit. The judges were impressed with the overall standard of work, and said it was almost impossible to make the final decisions.

The 30 winners were then each commissioned to illustrate a specific page of the book, and took part in two full-day workshops with a professional illustrator. There was then an exhibition of all the work at the View Two Gallery, Mathew Street, from 20th to 22nd August 2003.

We are especially grateful to all the teachers who encouraged the children to take part in the competition.

The 30 winners are pupils at the following schools in Liverpool: Abbots Lea School, All Saints RC Junior, Blessed Sacrament Infants, Broadgreen High School, King David High, Liverpool Bluecoat School, Monksdown Primary School, Northway County Primary, Our Lady's Bishop Eaton, Our Lady's of Reconciliation, Pleasant Street Primary, St. Cleopas JMI, St. Francis of Assisi, St. Hilda's Croxteth, and Springwood School.

Unfortunately, because of other commitments, one of the talented competition winners – Hannah Brellisford – could not finish her illustration and so does not appear in the book.

Paul Lee
age 15
Front cover

Callum Strode,
age 10
p4-5

Lauren
Duckworth, 7
p6

Tommy
Newman, age 7
p7

Alex Cook,
age 12
p8-9

Paul Gibson,
age 10
p10

Guy Cohen,
age 13
p11

Peter King,
age 7
p12-13

Olivia Hansen-
Bruder, age 10
p14

Tom Currie,
age 10
p15

Leigh
Fitzpatrick, 12
p16-17

Mary Edgar
age 10
p18

Sophie Wilson
age 7
p19

Caitlin Murney
age 7
p20

Natalie Fowler
age 14
p21

James Killick
age 12
p22

Andrew Price
age 11
p23

Danielle Ward
age 11
p24-25

Suzie Morris
age 13
p26

Gemma Fearon
age 8
p27

Helen
Robertshaw, 14
p28-29

Kaine Jones
age 5
p30

Lacey Littlemore,
age 6
p31

Vlad Paraoan
age 11
p32-33

Amanda Childs
age 12
p34-35 (top)

Ashleigh
Despoti, 12
p34-35 (bottom)

Thomas
McDonough, 6
p36-37

Oliver Padget
age 12
p38-39

Ste Daly,
age 15
p40-41

Marie Mairs
workshop leader

47

Last word

Hello, I want to take this opportunity to congratulate St George's Hall and everyone who worked so hard to make this marvellous book a reality.

The making of the book is a story in itself and is a testament to the amazing creativity in this great cultural city of ours. In our Year of Learning this project has been a beacon to show how education can help unlock so many doors of opportunity.

The fact that more than 1,100 pupils entered the picture competition to bring this book to life, shows just how much passion there is in this city for art and literature.

But it also says much more about the culture of participation, which is truly alive and kicking in the World in One City.

I know the judges were overawed by the quality of the work; debating the choice of the 30 young artists to commission for these pages was very difficult. I guess they got a glimpse of what it's like to be a Capital of Culture judge!

Once again publishers Garlic Press have done Liverpool proud; this beautiful book is further evidence of Liverpool's cultural status.

I'd also like to thank the generous sponsor of this book, JP Jacobs Charitable Trust, and those companies who sponsored the competition.

And last, but not least, thanks to the author Arabella McIntyre-Brown, whose story of Liverpool's Chinese dragon is helping to breathe fire back into the belly of St George's Hall – just as it is undergoing an £18m refurbishment to make it ready for a European Capital of Culture and the future to follow 2008.

So, enjoy the read and I'm sure that after you've put it down you will, like me, hope there are many more adventures for Xiaolong, the dragon of St George's Hall.

Sue Woodward
Creative Director of Liverpool – European Capital of Culture 2008